Dear Parents:

Congratulations! Your child is taking the first steps on an exciting journey. The destination? Independent reading!

STEP INTO READING® will help your child get there. The program offers five steps to reading success. Each step includes fun stories and colorful art or photographs. In addition to original fiction and books with favorite characters, there are Step into Reading Non-Fiction Readers, Phonics Readers and Boxed Sets, Sticker Readers, and Comic Readers—a complete literacy program with something to interest every child.

Learning to Read, Step by Step!

Ready to Read **Preschool–Kindergarten**
• big type and easy words • rhyme and rhythm • picture clues
For children who know the alphabet and are eager to begin reading.

Reading with Help **Preschool–Grade 1**
• basic vocabulary • short sentences • simple stories
For children who recognize familiar words and sound out new words with help.

Reading on Your Own **Grades 1–3**
• engaging characters • easy-to-follow plots • popular topics
For children who are ready to read on their own.

Reading Paragraphs **Grades 2–3**
• challenging vocabulary • short paragraphs • exciting stories
For newly independent readers who read simple sentences with confidence.

Ready for Chapters **Grades 2–4**
• chapters • longer paragraphs • full-color art
For children who want to take the plunge into chapter books but still like colorful pictures.

STEP INTO READING® is designed to give every child a successful reading experience. The grade levels are only guides; children will progress through the steps at their own speed, developing confidence in their reading.

Remember, a lifetime love of reading sta

Visit us on the Web!
StepIntoReading.com
rhcbooks.com

Educators and librarians, for a variety of teaching tools, visit us at RHTeachersLibrarians.com

ISBN 978-1-5247-6889-8 (trade) — ISBN 978-1-5247-6890-4 (lib. bdg.)

Printed in the United States of America 10 9 8 7 6 5 4 3 2 1

Random House Children's Books supports the First Amendment and celebrates the right to read.

STEP INTO READING®

nickelodeon

I LOVE King Dad!

based on the teleplay "A Striking Surprise"
by Jim Nolan

illustrated by Nneka Myers

Random House New York

Nella and Norma love to be with their father.

Every day is
an adventure
with King Dad.

Sometimes they
go to the beach.

Catch the ball, Nella!

Sometimes they
have tea parties.

Norma eats a cookie.

<u>Yum!</u>

When King Dad's band plays, they really rock!

Nella dances and dances.

Nella plays gobletball.
Her friends are
on her team.

King Dad cheers.

Hooray for Nella!

Nella also likes
to bowl with
King Dad.

Oh, no!
Some impkins
stop the game.
They take the
bowling balls!

The impkins roll
the balls everywhere!

Nella becomes a knight!

Her armor sparkles.

She shoots an arrow.
A ribbon is tied
to the arrow.

The ribbon stops
the rolling balls!

Nella saved the game!

King Dad hugs her.

When the day is over, King Dad, Norma, and Nella go home.

King Dad tucks
Norma into
her crib.

He reads Nella a story.

Nella loves King Dad!
And King Dad
loves Nella.